Enjoy the Adventure!

Praise for *The Adventures of Fuzzy and Buzzy*

"Kids will love learning about pollination along with a hungry bear who is befriended by a busy—and forgiving—bee. *The Adventures of Fuzzy and Buzzy* will entertain kids while also helping them get over their fear of bees. At a time when it's more important than ever for children to develop an appreciation for the interconnections within the natural world, this is a wonderful addition to a child's bookshelf."

—Lilace Mellin Guignard, author of *When Everything Beyond the Walls Is Wild: Being a Woman Outdoors in America*

"A charming and timely tale that will help kids understand and appreciate how creatures depend upon one another."

—Sean B. Carroll, biologist and author of *The Serengeti Rules*

"What a great book by one of my most enthusiastic students ever. It teaches kids (and their parents) about a really serious and important topic but does it in such a fun and creative way."

—Steven Stein, ecology professor at Mansfield University of PA

"A sweet and caring friendship that will touch the hearts of young children. Timely and sure to spark interest in the delicate balance found in nature."

—Mary Ann Yannetti, retired elementary educator

"This book, *The Adventures of Fuzzy and Buzzy*, is amazing. Being a retired elementary teacher, I love the book, the illustrations, and all the lessons throughout the book. I know the children will love it also. The story line is just what is being discussed by communities today: save the bees, which children are afraid of. This will give them a new understanding of bees and why we need them. Also, how friendships develop plus many more lessons. I would recommend this book to all the children and teachers, especially science teachers, at the elementary level."

—Carol McCaskey, retired teacher

"I'm a teacher, and I like books that teach kids something. Josh Brandstadter's *The Adventures of Fuzzy and Buzzy* does that. Readers learn about biology, the importance of bees, the effects of our behaviors, and how we can help. Plus, the story is fun and will get kids thinking early about natural processes and friends that are different—always a good thing. Read it!"

—Jimmy Guignard, professor of English and author of *Pedaling the Sacrifice Zone: Teaching, Writing, and Living Above the Marcellus Shale*

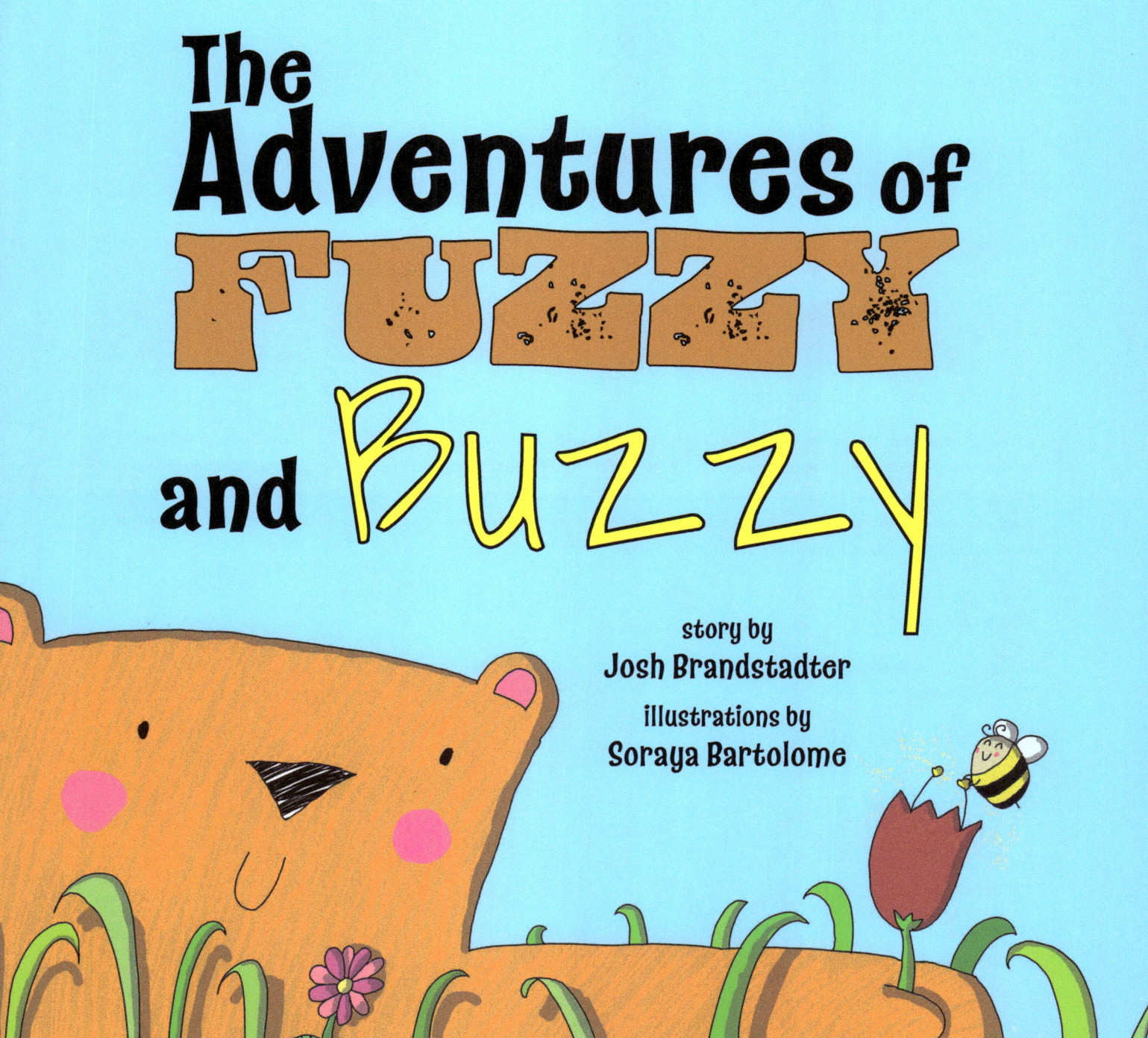

Copyright © 2021 by Josh Brandstadter

All rights reserved. No part of this book may be reproduced in any form or by any electronic or mechanical means, or the facilitation thereof, including information storage and retrieval systems, without permission in writing from the publisher, except in the case of brief quotations published in articles and reviews. Any educational institution wishing to photocopy part or all of the work for classroom use, or individual researchers who would like to obtain permission to reprint the work for educational purposes, should contact the publisher.

ISBN: 978-1-951565-44-2
LCCN: 2020925274

Designed by Michael Hardison
Production managed by Christina Kann

Printed in the United States of America

Published by
Brandylane Publishers, Inc.
5 S. 1st Street
Richmond, Virginia 23219

brandylanepublishers.com

*For Emery and Ayla—
May your passion for nature bloom
as you grow and experience the world around you.*

Fuzzy was a **bear**,
as you can plainly see.

Fuzzy had just woken up from
a long winter hibernation,
and he was very hungry.

He decided to look for something to eat.

Across the forest, Buzzy was hard at work.
You can probably tell that Buzzy was a *bee*.

She was busy collecting nectar
from flowers to make honey.
After collecting all the nectar she
could carry, she headed home.

Meanwhile, Fuzzy was still trying to
find something to eat.
He was not having much luck.

He tried some grass, but it was **TOO BITTER.**

He tried some bark, but it was **too hard**.

He tried some dirt, but it was too dry.

He even tried a **smelly** old sock . . .
It just tasted like **dirty feet**.

Just when Fuzzy was about to give up,
his nose began to **twitch** and his stomach began to **SPiN**.
He smelled something delicious, and he knew just what it was.

It was a beehive! Inside was golden, sticky, sweet **HONEY!**
Fuzzy started gobbling it up.

While Fuzzy was enjoying the honey,
Buzzy flew back toward the hive, singing her favorite song:

I love to buzz, buzz, buzz from flower to flower,

Gathering up nectar as I go.

I'm happy to help my flower friends

Because without me, nothing would grow.

By the time Buzzy made it back to her hive,
Fuzzy had eaten a **TREMENDOUS** amount of honey.
He was sitting under the hive,
and his belly was **round and full.**

Buzzy flew in circles around Fuzzy's big head.
Fuzzy watched her go
'round and 'round and 'round.
All Buzzy's flying made Fuzzy very dizzy,
and he fell over with a loud **THUD!**
Buzzy landed on Fuzzy's nose and shouted,
"WHY ARE YOU EATING MY HONEY?"

Fuzzy, still trying to stop his head from spinning, replied, "I just woke up from a long winter's hibernation, and I was very hungry. I tried to eat grass, but it made my tongue tingle. I tried to eat dirt, but it made me thirsty. I tried to eat bark, but it hurt my teeth. I even tried eating a smelly old sock, but it tasted like dirty feet. When I smelled your honey, I knew I would like it!"

Buzzy gave Fuzzy a stern look and moved in closer.

Fuzzy had to cross his eyes to see Buzzy.

Buzzy was not happy, and for good reason.

Fuzzy had eaten almost all of her honey.

Fuzzy could tell he was in **BIG TROUBLE**.

He knew what he had to do.

"I'm sorry for eating your honey," said Fuzzy.
"If you teach me, I promise I will
help you make more honey."
He stuck out his finger to Buzzy.
Buzzy, pleased with the offer,
shook Fuzzy's finger with her
tiny bee leg and said,

"Okay, follow me!"

Buzzy showed Fuzzy the best flowers, and explained
how to tell when they were ready.
Then, she taught him how to gather nectar from
the flowers and carry it back to the hive.
Buzzy showed Fuzzy how to make nectar into HONEY.

They put mounds of nectar into their mouths,
then spat the STICKY liquid
into honeycombs inside the hive.
Fuzzy found this to be much more enjoyable
than chewing on dirty socks.

They worked until they had gathered enough nectar to replace all the honey that Fuzzy had eaten.
It had only taken Fuzzy minutes to eat all that honey, but it took them hours working together to collect enough nectar to fill the honeycombs.
What Fuzzy didn't realize was that it would take months for the nectar to finally turn into honey again!

Tired from all their hard work, Fuzzy and Buzzy both lay down on the ground under the hive.

"You know, collecting nectar is not all about making honey," said Buzzy, looking at Fuzzy with her tired bee eyes. Fuzzy replied, "What do you mean?"

"See that tree?" said Buzzy. She pointed to her hive and the tree it was hanging from. "That tree would not be here without bees and other **pollinators** like me."

Fuzzy raised his eyebrows, looking confused, so Buzzy explained. "When bees gather nectar, we also help pollinate the plants. That helps them make seeds so new plants can grow," said Buzzy.

"We helped grow this forest, and other pollinators like me helped grow all of the forests of the world."

Amazed, Fuzzy sat up.

"You mean I was a pollinator today, like you?"

Buzzy nodded.

"And I helped pollinate the flowers today, giving them a chance to make seeds that will grow into other plants and flowers?" said Fuzzy, excited.

Smiling, Buzzy nodded again. "I have a song I like to sing when I am gathering nectar. Want to hear it?"

"Yes, of course!" said Fuzzy.

And Buzzy sang her song:

I love to buzz, buzz, buzz from flower to flower,

Gathering up nectar as I go.

I'm happy to help my flower friends

Because without me, nothing would grow.

Fuzzy and Buzzy sang the song together, over and over,
as they watched the sun set over the horizon.
They might have been an unlikely pair,
but just like the many flowers they helped pollinate,
their friendship had **bloomed.**

Bees and other pollinators face a world that is getting harder and harder to live in. They are being killed by pesticides. The plants and flowers they pollinate are being removed and replaced with homes and other buildings. Climates around the world are changing due to human influence. All of this is putting pressure on our pollinators.

WHAT CAN WE DO TO HELP?

Plant native wildflowers.

Bees and other pollinators love all flowers, but they really go for the wildflowers that naturally grow in their region. Search the internet for the best ones to plant in your area, and grow some in your yard.

Go pesticide-free.

Use natural methods for controlling pests around your house. A quick internet search will provide many suggestions for alternative materials. Some of the most common natural pest control substances are vinegar and spices. Find the right combination, and use these instead of harmful pesticides.

Build a pollinator hotel.

You can create a great home for many native pollinators in your area using old landscaping materials and wood. Give them a place to live and help prevent them from building their homes on or inside yours. It's a win-win for you and the pollinators!

Donate to an organization helping pollinators.

A number of different organizations are involved in setting up programs and teaching the public about the importance of protecting native pollinators. Many of these organizations accept donations through their websites. Run an internet search for organizations in your area, or go to www.pollinator.org to donate to Pollinator Partnership, the largest non-profit dedicated to the protection and promotion of pollinators and their ecosystems.

About the Author

JOSH BRANDSTADTER lives in Dover, Pennsylvania with his wife, Jamie; his children, Emery and Ayla; and his dog, Tom Petty. He is a science teacher at Dover Area High School and has always had a passion for nature. When he isn't in the classroom, you'll find him spending time with his family in the great outdoors.

About the Illustrator

SORAYA BARTOLOME was born in Córdoba in the South of Spain in 1982. She grew up in a family of artists, so she learned different painting techniques very soon in her mother's painting studio. In 1990, she began studying piano at the Music Conservatory of Córdoba, which would take ten years. When she finished her music studies and her studies at the Art Institute in Córdoba, she started to study a degree in musical education in the University Complutense of Madrid, and then pursued a musicology degree in the University Autónoma of Madrid. Since 2010, Soraya has been working in the field of adult education, which she combines with her musicology projects. Her interest in children's illustration has been cultivated from her infancy until today, and for this reason, in December of 2016, she decided to dedicate her time and her enthusiasm to becoming a professional children's illustrator. During this time she has worked as an illustrator on projects in the US and UK. Her illustrations are adorable, colorful, and tender, with a strong personality that is part of the sweet world of colors in Soraya's drawings.

CPSIA information can be obtained
at www.ICGtesting.com
Printed in the USA
BVHW022109110421
604661BV00001B/1